THE WAVE OF THE SEA-WOLF

For Dilys, Dorothy, and Dinah

Clarion Books • a Houghton Mifflin Company imprint • 215 Park Avenue South, New York, NY 10003 • Text and illustrations copyright © 1994 by David Wisniewski • The illustrations for this book were executed in cut paper (Chrome-arama, Color-Aid, and Canson charcoal papers). • The text was set in 14/18-pt. Simoncini Garamond • All rights reserved. • For information about permission to reproduce selections from this book, write to Permissions, Houghton Mifflin Company, 215 Park Avenue South, New York, NY 10003. • Printed in the USA • Library of Congress Cataloging-in-Publication Data • Wisniewski, David. The wave of the Sea-Wolf / written and illustrated by David Wisniewski. p. cm. Summary: Kchokeen, a Tlingit princess, is rescued from drowning by a guardian spirit that later enables Kchokeen to summon a great wave and save her people from hostile strangers. ISBN 0-395-66478-0 [1. Fairy tales. 2. Tlingit Indians—Fiction. 3. Indians of North America—Northwest, Pacific—Fiction.] I. Title. PZ8.W754Wat 1994 [E]—dc20 93-18265 CIP AC
HOR 10 9 8 7 6 5 4 3 2 1

Photography of cut-paper illustrations by Lee Salsbery

THE WAVE OF THE
SEA-WOLF

STORY AND PICTURES BY DAVID WISNIEWSKI

Clarion Books • New York

From the misty land between sea and mountain, the tops of the tallest trees can rarely be seen. But when the clouds part, a marvelous thing can be observed against the sky—a war canoe, trapped in the trunk of a lofty cedar.

The tree has grown around the battered craft, lifting it higher with each passing year. Though its painted prow is splintered, the canoe seems to sail proudly on an airy ocean of green and gray.

How did it come to rest in this unlikely place? The few who remember will tell you this. . . .

Long ago in the land of the Tlingit, there lived a young princess named Kchokeen. She was the only daughter in a family of many sons, and was admired for her intelligence as well as her beauty.

One day, Kchokeen and her friends planned to gather salmon-berries. The fresh fruit would be welcome after the winter diet of dried fish.

"You may go," said her mother, "but stay away from the mouth of the bay. Great waves suddenly appear there, and many lives have been lost."

"Perhaps Gonakadet—the Sea-Wolf—makes those waves!" said Kchokeen. "Anyone who sees Gonakadet is sure to receive great wealth and honor!"

"And what use are wealth and honor after drowning?" replied her mother. "Hear me: do not go there."

The girls beached their canoe on the far shore of the bay and entered the forest. Their faces fell when they saw bushes bearing unripe fruit.

"Let's keep walking," said Kchokeen. "Perhaps riper berries are ahead, where the trees let more sunlight through."

"But that is at the mouth of the bay," one of her friends protested.

"Mother warned us about the water," reasoned Kchokeen, "not the land," and she led the way.

The girls found plenty of bright yellow fruit. Her basket filled, the princess climbed onto the great trunk of a fallen tree to survey the calm water.

"I see no danger here," she declared.

At that moment the rotten wood beneath her gave way, and Kchokeen plunged into darkness.

From the bottom of the hollow trunk, Kchokeen gazed upward at the anxious faces of her friends.

"I'm not hurt," she called, "but I can't get out. Go back to the village. Fetch a rope and one of my brothers."

"Should one of us stay with you?"

"No," said Kchokeen. "Two can paddle faster than one."

The girls began to cry. "We can't just leave you!" they sobbed.

"That is foolish," the princess chided them. "How can you come back with help if you don't go away? Now, hurry!"

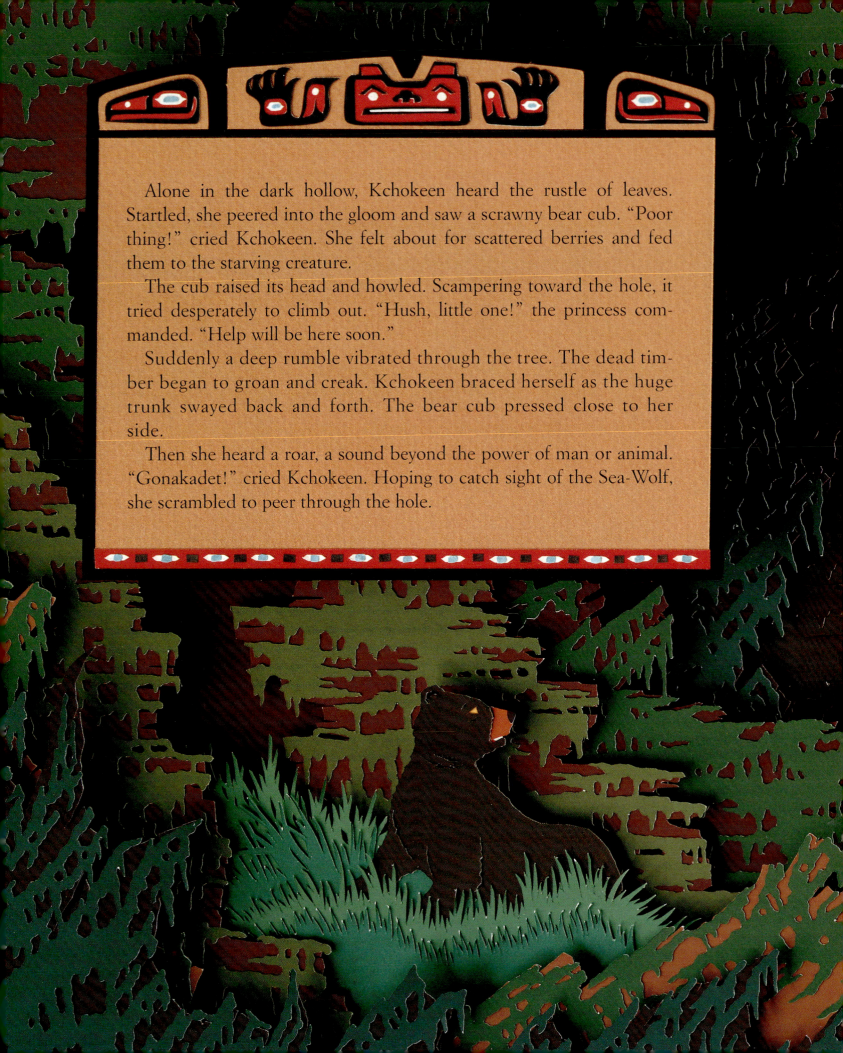

Alone in the dark hollow, Kchokeen heard the rustle of leaves. Startled, she peered into the gloom and saw a scrawny bear cub. "Poor thing!" cried Kchokeen. She felt about for scattered berries and fed them to the starving creature.

The cub raised its head and howled. Scampering toward the hole, it tried desperately to climb out. "Hush, little one!" the princess commanded. "Help will be here soon."

Suddenly a deep rumble vibrated through the tree. The dead timber began to groan and creak. Kchokeen braced herself as the huge trunk swayed back and forth. The bear cub pressed close to her side.

Then she heard a roar, a sound beyond the power of man or animal. "Gonakadet!" cried Kchokeen. Hoping to catch sight of the Sea-Wolf, she scrambled to peer through the hole.

A frothing wall of water was bearing down on them. The wave crashed into the trunk and sent it spinning through the forest. Great booms shuddered through the wood as it collided with rocks and trees. Kchokeen clapped her hands over her ears against the grinding and splintering. She was sure their clumsy vessel was being torn apart.

At last, the huge tree ground to a halt. Salt water gushed into the hollow, lifting Kchokeen and the cub to the top. They clambered out, gasping for breath, as the wave surged past them.

The waters receded slowly. The unhappy cub drew near Kchokeen as evening fell. That night, both shivered with cold and hunger. Unable to sleep, the princess gazed at the shimmering landscape. And there, in the reflection of the moon and the shadows of trees, she saw Gonakadet.

Kchokeen marveled at the vision. She remembered how her brothers had kept lonely watch in the wilderness, praying for the appearance of *yek,* the mighty spirits that granted wisdom and ability. Sometimes girls also saw these spirits and were blessed by them. But no girl had ever seen Gonakadet.

Overcome with awe and wonder, Kchokeen fell to her knees. The moon and stars swam before her eyes. Yet she smiled, for she knew that a great gift would be bestowed upon her. She was smiling still when her father and brothers rescued her the next morning.

Thereafter, Kchokeen could foretell the giant waves that marked Gonakadet's travels at the mouth of the bay. The trembling of the earth and the sound of the sea told her much, but it was the howl of the bear that meant a wave was coming. The fishermen were grateful for her predictions, because now they could travel the waters in safety. The village prospered, and the people accorded Kchokeen great honor and wealth.

One morning Kchokeen saw a huge black creature emerge from the mists of the bay. Its back sprouted great trees from which flapped enormous white wings.

"Is this not Raven, the Creator of All?" Kchokeen gasped. She turned away quickly, for to see Raven with unshielded eyes was to be changed to stone.

She ran to the village, where she found her father calming the people. "What you see is but a ship," he said. "It contains men, not unlike ourselves, from a land across the water. They come bearing goodwill and a stock of useful wonders; they have traded with villages to the south."

Kchokeen was comforted by her father's words. But she felt uneasy during the weeks that followed, as her people traded furs for the strong metal tools of the strangers.

One evening Kchokeen's father returned from the black ship in haste. "Great danger is upon us!" he shouted. "Leave your belongings and flee!"

No sooner had the people departed than loud booms pierced the twilight. As Kchokeen and the elders watched in horror, the long houses collapsed in splinters.

"Why is this happening?" asked Kchokeen.

"The foreigners demanded more furs than we had," her father told her angrily. "They ordered us to trap many more. I refused, for animals cannot be hunted without mercy and reverence. And so, to punish us, they are using their weapons to destroy our homes!" He turned to her. "You have been blessed with wisdom and power beyond your years. What can be done?"

Kchokeen gazed somberly at the burning village. "I shall ask the Sea-Wolf."

Those aboard the black ship did not see how the earth shook that night. In the morning, few noticed the deepening swells that slapped the vessel's hull, or the bear that began to howl in the ruined village.

Then a war canoe bolted toward the mouth of the bay. Propelled by a dozen warriors, the craft carried Kchokeen and bundles of costly fur. At once the black ship raised anchor and pursued it. There was a loud boom, and the sea erupted about the fleeing canoe. But this time the boom was answered by a roar.

The wave of the Sea-Wolf rose like a mountain behind the black ship
and fell upon it with the fury of a living thing. In an instant, the vessel
disappeared in a mass of churning foam.

Then the wave thundered on to engulf the canoe.

The war canoe flew on the rising crest of Gonakadet's wave, skimming the treetops as it entered the flooded forest. Kchokeen's kinsmen, guiding the craft, could not avoid the cedar that loomed ahead of them.

Their speed was so great that the prow split the tree apart. The canoe was wedged firmly in the cleft, and its occupants rode out the flood in safety.

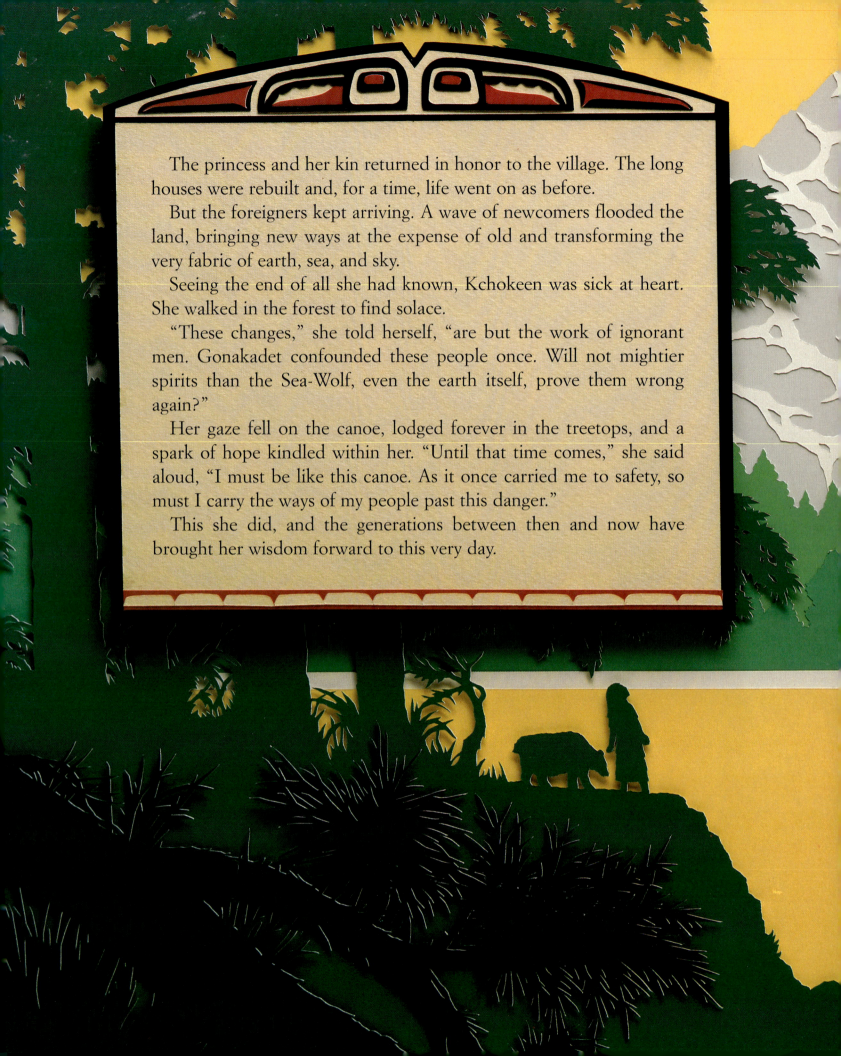

The princess and her kin returned in honor to the village. The long houses were rebuilt and, for a time, life went on as before.

But the foreigners kept arriving. A wave of newcomers flooded the land, bringing new ways at the expense of old and transforming the very fabric of earth, sea, and sky.

Seeing the end of all she had known, Kchokeen was sick at heart. She walked in the forest to find solace.

"These changes," she told herself, "are but the work of ignorant men. Gonakadet confounded these people once. Will not mightier spirits than the Sea-Wolf, even the earth itself, prove them wrong again?"

Her gaze fell on the canoe, lodged forever in the treetops, and a spark of hope kindled within her. "Until that time comes," she said aloud, "I must be like this canoe. As it once carried me to safety, so must I carry the ways of my people past this danger."

This she did, and the generations between then and now have brought her wisdom forward to this very day.

A Note

On the Pacific Northwest coast of North America, a ruggedly beautiful strip of land runs from the mouth of Washington State's Columbia River northward to Alaska's Yakutat Bay. Forbidding peaks born of volcano and earthquake loom alongside great valleys and fjords cut by the retreating glaciers of the Ice Age. Mighty storms and dense fogs sweep the area, and more than 260 inches of rain fall each year.

This downpour created the continent's greatest coniferous rainforest: great stands of moss-covered spruce, fir, hemlock, and cedar that sheltered large populations of bear, cougar, deer, and elk. So dense were these woods that the first settlers had to turn to the adjacent ocean for sustenance.

The coastal waters abounded with whales, walrus, and sea lions, as well as halibut, flounder, and sturgeon. Salmon entered the rivers each summer to spawn. So great were their numbers that one early European explorer claimed he crossed a river by walking on their backs.

By 2000 B.C., the coastal peoples had developed a distinct culture. They specialized in fishing and stored their catch for winter use by drying, smoking, or packing in fish oil. The forest timber, especially red cedar, was crafted into communal homes, impressive dugout canoes, and towering totem poles. Trade began, and a stratified society of nobles, commoners, and slaves evolved.

Eventually, seven Indian nations emerged. Grouped by language, they are the Coast Salish (SAY lish), Nootka (NOOT kuh), Kwakiutl (kwah kee OO tul), Bella Coola (BEL luh KOO luh), Haida (HYE duh), Tsimshian (TSIM shee un), and Tlingit (KLING git). The Tlingit live the farthest north, on coastline and islands deeply etched with bays and inlets. One of these, Lituya Bay, inspired much of this story.

On July 4, 1786, the Tlingit community was astonished to see two white-winged vessels enter the bay. At first, villagers thought they were visions of Raven or *Yehlh*, the creator spirit of the Pacific Northwest peoples. They peered at the spectacle through the rolled leaves of skunk cabbage, to avoid the risk of being changed to stone. When they found out that the apparitions were mere ships, under the command of French explorer Count Jean François de la Perouse, they initiated the trade of sea otter fur for metal tools.

But the villagers were still impressed with the ships' initial entry into Lituya Bay. The Tlingit regarded the entrance to the bay with dread because of its treacherous currents. Native belief held that the turbulence was caused by Kay-Lituya, a froglike monster that lurked in underwater caves. De la Perouse's forces fell victim to the fabled beast; a mapping expedition was sucked into the churning waves of the bay's outflow, and twenty-one men were drowned.

Like many other stories created by indigenous peoples to explain natural phenomena, the myth of Kay-Lituya reflects an acute awareness of the earth's forces. Later scientific investigation often reveals more information about the actual cause.

On July 9, 1958, a massive earthquake wracked Lituya Bay. From the 3,000-foot cliffs surrounding the water 90 million tons of rock plunged down, producing a wave 1,740 feet high, the tallest in recorded history. After the cataclysm, geologists discovered a fault lying across the mouth of the bay. When activated by earthquakes, it triggers huge avalanches and underwater disturbances.

Animals often show by their behavior that they sense imminent earthquake activity. Before the great Alaska temblor of 1964, bears woke from hibernation and exhibited frantic behavior. This little-understood response is being studied as a way of predicting earthquakes.

For the purposes of this story, I substituted the Tlingit legend of Gonakadet (go NOK uh det), also known as the Sea-Wolf, for the destructive Kay-Lituya. Though capable of drowning those who broke tribal taboos, Gonakadet was primarily viewed as a bringer of wealth and good fortune. Kchokeen sees this creature in an inadvertent "vision quest," a search for the *yek* or guiding spirit that would direct her life and grant her new abilities.

The art of the Pacific Northwest Indian nations is extremely complex and sophisticated. It adorns everyday objects as well as the implements of ritual. The decorations around the text blocks in this book are derived from this style.

Some of the early European and Russian voyagers to the region were impressed by native culture and truly fulfilled their mission as explorers. Unfortunately, they opened the way for others who viewed the land and sea as infinitely renewable sources of profit. Although the Pacific Northwest peoples were also concerned with amassing wealth, they brought to the process a profound respect for the environment that produced it.

The newcomers' attitude was almost fatal to the area's environment and native cultures. In the mid-1780s, the sea otter fur trade was in its prime. By 1820, the animal was almost extinct. In 1850, whaling and sealing were at their height. By 1870, so few whales remained that the industry collapsed, and sealing ended thirty years later. Logging decimated the ancient rainforest and the fragile ecosystem it maintained; controversy between timber and environmental interests continues to this day.

Like native populations in many parts of the world, the Tlingit had no defense against the new diseases carried by the foreigners. Influenza, smallpox, and measles reduced some village populations by 90 percent. Prohibited by the newcomers from speaking their language and engaging in the rituals of their ancestors, the people were separated from their culture. Recently the Tlingit and other peoples of the Pacific Northwest have made valiant, successful strides toward preserving their language and cultural traditions. It is to be hoped that their magnificent natural environment will be preserved as well.